The Cruise of the Noah's Ark

David Cory

Copyright © 2023 Culturea Editions
Text and cover : © public domain
Edition : Culturea (Hérault, 34)
Contact : infos@culturea.fr
Print in Germany by Books on Demand
Design and layout : Derek Murphy
Layout : Reedsy (https://reedsy.com/)
ISBN : 9791041827749
Légal deposit : July 2023

The Cruise Of The Noah's Ark

ALL ABOARD!

A stands for Animal, Ant or Ape,

Quite different in spelling as well as in shape.

"Oh, dear!" sighed Marjorie, "I'm tired of writing in this old copy book. What's the use of making the letters just like the copy, anyhow? Mother doesn't. Her capitals are very different."

B stands for Bruin, Bee or Bug—

The Bee has a sting and the Bear has a hug!

"Oh, dear!" sighed Marjorie again, while she rested her head on her arm and looked over at the Noah's Ark.

And then, all of a sudden, something very strange happened. Mr. Noah came out of his little Ark and said, "You had better come with us, for it is going to rain for 40 days and 40 nights, and goodness knows where this nursery will be by the end of that time; probably floating about, half full of water, in the apple orchard."

"Do you really mean it?" asked Marjorie, gazing anxiously out of the window at the rain which was falling in torrents.

"I certainly do," replied Mr. Noah.

And then Mrs. Noah poked her head out of a little window in the Ark. "Listen to Mr. Noah, my dear, for he was certainly right the first time, and why shouldn't he be now?"

Mr. Noah smiled and walked across the table towards a little yellow hen. "Shoo," he cried, as the contrary fowl tried to dodge around a toy automobile. "Shoo there. You know you can't swim like Mrs. Duck, so why don't you have some sense and get aboard out of harm's way?"

As he finished speaking, water began to pour over the windowsill, and soon the nursery floor was ankle deep. Marjorie stood on a chair and, climbing upon the table, walked over to the Ark. On her way she picked up her rag doll, Maria Jane, and the little toy automobile.

"Hurry, my dear," cried Mr. Noah, "here comes the water over the edge of the table."

As it was, Maria Jane was splashed a bit, and so was the automobile before it was pushed through the narrow doorway, for the Ark was rolling from side to side in rather a dangerous manner.

"Make everything tight. Close the hatches and the portholes!" commanded Capt. Noah (for now that they were actually afloat, this seemed the proper title for him), and in a few minutes it was comfortable and snug inside.

And then, all of a sudden, a big wave carried them over the windowsill and out into the garden. But it didn't look very much like the garden, for only the tops of the rose bushes could be seen, and the roses rested on the water like pond lilies. And then, away sailed the Ark, across the garden, over the fence, down the road, until it reached an open space.

"The ocean!" cried Mrs. Noah.

"Nonsense!" exclaimed Marjorie, "I beg your pardon, Mrs. Noah, I mean it's Uncle Spencer's meadow. Why, there's Tim! Let's save him!" And Marjorie ran down to the lower floor of the Ark and commenced to unfasten the door.

"Careful, my dear," cried Capt. Noah. "What are you about?"

"Oh, hurry, Captain," begged Marjorie, "Tim, Uncle Spencer's dog, is in the water and I want to bring him aboard."

"Here, mates, bring me a life line," shouted Capt. Noah, and in less time than I can take to tell it the line was thrown to the little dog, who managed to catch hold of it with his teeth just in time, for the Ark was going at a tremendous rate of speed.

"Don't haul in too fast," advised Capt. Noah, as his three sons began pulling in the rope, "or he'll be drawn under the water and smothered before we can get him aboard."

At last, the little dog was landed safely on the deck. Everybody ran away from him to avoid getting a shower bath as he shook himself again and again.

"Well, you've all proved to be brave lifesavers," said Mrs. Noah. "Now I'll give him some warm milk and dry him by the kitchen fire, or he may get a severe cold. Goodness knows what would happen if he gave it to the other animals and they all got to sneezing and coughing at the same time."

And then the good woman took the little dog down into the hold of the Ark, where the pantry and kitchen were, and he was soon fast asleep by the stove, none the worse for his wetting.

It was now time for supper, so Mrs. Noah busied herself preparing the evening meal, while Capt. Noah and his three sons, Ham, Shem and Japheth, fed the animals. This was not an easy matter, for each animal had a different taste, and the fodder had to be carefully measured so as to give each one enough and no more.

The elephant ate almost a bale of hay for each meal, and the lion ate about twenty large Delmonico steaks.

"It's lucky we haven't a whale on board," said Capt. Noah, as he rolled a bale of hay up to Mrs. Elephant, at the same time warning Ham not to give the lion a sirloin steak by mistake.

"You might feed the pigs, too," he added, wiping his forehead with a red-bordered handkerchief. "They seem to like you, Ham. I guess they consider you one of the family!"

Marjorie thought the rabbits were very pretty, but just as she was about to play a game of hide and go seek with them, the supper bell rang, and as soon as the three Noah boys had washed their hands and combed their hair they came to the table. Shem pulled out his mother's chair and Ham politely helped Marjorie into hers.

It was all very interesting to the little girl, and when Mrs. Noah looked over at her and said, in a motherly way, "I always wanted a little girl of my own," Marjorie felt quite at home.

"Thank you, ma'am," she said, "but I think you have very nice boys!"

After the supper table was cleared and the dishes washed, Mrs. Noah and Marjorie went up on deck, where they found Capt. Noah contentedly smoking his pipe. The three boys were having a merry time with the little dog. The rain had stopped and the sky was full of stars.

"I don't know how much of a rainfall we have had this time," said Capt. Noah, "but it must have been pretty heavy, for there seems to be as much water around as there was when it rained for 40 days and 40 nights."

And then, all of a sudden, a harsh, grating noise was heard and everybody jumped up. "Have we struck a rock?" inquired Mrs. Noah anxiously.

"I don't know," answered Capt. Noah, peering over the side. "I can't see bottom."

Suddenly the Ark stopped altogether.

"Guess we're aground now, all right," said Japheth. "It's too dark to tell much about it, though."

"No, it isn't!" cried a deep, gurgling voice, and their astonished eyes saw the head of a whale rise above the bow.

"I have a passenger for you," continued the whale. "He doesn't like his present mode of travel, so I'm going to ship him over to you."

"How do you know we want him?" inquired Capt. Noah, going forward to investigate. "We have a pretty full house as things are. And, besides, he might be a Jonah."

"That's just who he is!" spouted the whale, with a gleeful gurgle, and before any one could say "Jack Robinson!" Mr. Jonah appeared upon the deck of the Ark, and with a swish of his great tail the whale disappeared in the darkness.

"Sorry if I am intruding," said Mr. Jonah apologetically, "but the truth is it was so dark and uncomfortable inside that whale that I would have had nervous prostration had I been obliged to remain there another minute."

"Well," said Mrs. Noah, slowly, looking Mr. Jonah over and seeing that he wasn't such a bad looking person, after all, although a trifle damp, "we'll see how we get along."

By this time Marjorie began to feel tired.

"Would you mind," she said, turning to Mrs. Noah, "if I went to bed? I feel so sleepy, and it's long past Maria Jane's bedtime, I'm sure."

"Come right along with me," answered Mrs. Noah kindly.

"Good night, all," said Marjorie, following Mrs. Noah into the Ark.

"You shall sleep in the room next to mine," said Mrs. Noah, turning to the little girl with a smile as she led the way into a pretty bedroom. "Would you like me to unfasten your dress for you?"

"I think I can manage that," replied Marjorie, "but if you wouldn't mind, I'd like to have you wait and tuck me in bed after I've said my prayers. I can't very well tuck in the sheets at the side after I'm once in."

So good, kind, motherly Mrs. Noah tucked in the little girl and kissed her good night, and in a few minutes she was fast asleep, with her arms tightly clasped around her rag doll, Maria Jane.

COCK-A-DOODLE-DO

"Cock-a-Doodle-Do,

My Master's lost a shoe,

But what's the use of an excuse

A rubber boot'll do."

Marjorie leaped out of bed and ran over to the window to see where the Ark had drifted during the night.

To her surprise it was aground on the roof of a big barn.

And, goodness me! Didn't the weathercock look handsome, with his gilt feathers shining brightly in the rays of the morning sun as he turned to and fro with every little change of wind.

"Good morning," said Marjorie. "Isn't it a beautiful day?"

"I don't feel sure about anything," replied the weathercock. "I used to be a jolly weathercock, but now, with all this water around, I feel more like a lighthouse."

"Then why didn't you warn us off the reef—I mean the roof?" asked Marjorie.

"I did, but everybody was asleep and paid no attention to me."

And just then the wind came in a sudden gust and the weathercock flew around to face it.

"Goodness," he cried, "I believe it's going to rain again."

"Ahoy, there," shouted Capt. Noah from the deck below, "tell that gilt rooster I'm going to shove off. If he wants to come aboard he'd better be quick about it."

"Would you like to come with us?" asked Marjorie. "I'd like to have you. I once read about a very nice weathercock in 'Old Mother Goose.'"

"Thank you, I think I will," replied the weathercock, hopping nimbly on to the flagpole of the Ark. "I shall feel more at home here now that the green meadows have turned into an ocean. A barn is no place for a rooster when the water is above the hayloft."

Marjorie had no time to answer, for just then the rain began to fall in torrents, making it necessary to close the window.

In a few minutes the Ark began to quiver and shake, and then, with a loud grating noise it slipped off the ridge of the roof and once more floated down the tide.

"Good-by, red barn, with your loft of hay,

We're off on a voyage to Far Away,"

crowed the weathercock. And then Marjorie waved her hand from behind the window pane and ran down to breakfast where in a few minutes the family were all seated around the table.

"What did you give the pigs for supper last night?" asked Capt. Noah, looking at Ham suspiciously.

"Why, father?" asked Ham, in a low voice.

"Because they don't seem well this morning."

"I gave them some green apples," said Ham.

"W-e-l-l," replied Capt. Noah, "don't know as that should make them ill?"

"I chased them 'round the deck."

"What in thunder did you do that for?" asked his father.

"I wanted to see them slide when they turned the corners," said Ham, sheepishly.

"Perhaps they were seasick," interposed Mrs. Noah, who began to feel sorry for Ham.

"Perhaps they weren't," said Capt. Noah, sternly. "I think, young man, you had better be locked up in the brig for the rest of the day and fed on bread and water. We can't afford to have any passengers abused by the crew," and then he turned to Marjorie and smiled, "even if one of the crew happens to be the captain's son."

And after that, poor Ham was solemnly marched up to the brig and locked in, much to Marjorie's regret, for she liked Ham very much, although he was the most mischievous of all Capt. Noah's sons.

It was still raining heavily, and as the wind was blowing quite a gale the sea became rough and the Ark began to roll from side to side.

Pretty soon the animals grew uneasy, and strange noises came from many parts of the boat.

The roar of the tiger mingled with the trumpeting of the elephant and the howling of the wolf made a dreadful discord with the bellowing of the buffalo.

Then the monkeys started to chatter, and the parrots to screech, the horses to neigh and the pigs to squeak, the cows to moo and the donkeys to bray, the wild hyena to laugh and the little lambs to bleat.

But luckily toward evening the storm went down, and if it had not I guess Mrs. Noah would have gone crazy.

The dove, which was the most quiet and peaceful of all the passengers, perched herself on Marjorie's shoulder.

"You shall sleep in my cabin," said the little girl, stroking its glossy neck. "I'm sure you'd never get a wink of sleep if you had to stay below decks to-night."

Toward evening the weather grew calm, and after supper the rain having stopped, Marjorie went on deck for some fresh air. The weathercock, on seeing the dove perched on the little girl's shoulder, called out politely, "Good evening, ladies."

"Aren't you glad it cleared off?" asked Marjorie, looking up with a smile.

"Indeed I am," he replied, swinging around on one toe like a dancer.

"Isn't he graceful?" cooed the dove in Marjorie's ear.

"S-s-sh!" she answered. "Don't let him hear you. He might get conceited."

"What are you talking about down there?" asked the weathercock.

"Oh, nothing in particular," answered the dove. "I was just receiving a little advice from Marjorie."

"Well, you probably won't use it," said the weathercock. "So you might just as well hand it over to me."

"My, how curious you are!" laughed Marjorie.

"You'd be, too," answered the weathercock, "if you were in the habit of having the winds tell you each day what was going on. It's not so much curiosity as habit."

Just then Mrs. Noah called: "Marjorie, I think you'd better come in. It's too damp outside, my dear."

The cabin looked very cozy. Mrs. Noah was seated by the table knitting a pair of socks for the captain, and the three boys were writing in their copy books.

"I think, my dear," said Mrs. Noah, kindly, "it would be a good thing for you to do a little studying each day." So Marjorie seated herself at the table and Mrs. Noah opened a writing book and laid it before her. With a cry of surprise Marjorie turned to Mrs. Noah:

"Why, it's the very copy book I have at home!"

"'A stands for Animal, Ant or Ape,

Quite different in spelling as well as in shape.'"

"The very same," cried Marjorie again.

"See how well you can make the capital letters," suggested Mrs. Noah. "If you fill in this book nicely you can take it home with you and show your mother how well you employed your time aboard the Ark."

"Oh, thank you," cried Marjorie. "That will be lovely. Mother is always worrying about my handwriting. I shall try my best to improve."

Mrs. Noah then turned to look in Ham's book.

"That is not a very good 'C' you have just made," she said.

"Well, you see," answered Ham, with a laugh, "the sea is so rough that it made my 'C' rough, too."

Everybody laughed at Ham's witty excuse.

"What's all this levity about?" asked Capt. Noah, entering the cabin.

"Coo!" said the little dove,

"Coo!" said she,

"And they all lived together

In the big green tree."

"Hello!" exclaimed Capt. Noah, forgetting his own question, "the dove spouting poetry, eh? Well, we'll have to give an entertainment. There must be lots of talent on board. Plenty of material for a circus, anyhow."

"How jolly!" exclaimed Marjorie. "I'll make a ring to-morrow," said Japheth. "I've already trained one of the little pigs to walk on its hind legs," said Ham. "It's the white one with the pink nose."

"The elephant and I are great friends," added Shem. "I think he'd do anything I asked him. Tonight when I rolled up his bale of hay, he said, 'Hey, young man, look out for my toes!' And then he stood up on top of the bale on his hind legs just as they do in the circus. I'll bet I could make him do a lot of stunts."

"Just you wait until you see my wrestling monkeys," cried Ham. "I've taught two of them already. They'll be better than a moving picture show."

"My goodness, I think you have very clever boys," said Marjorie, who was tickled to death to think they were going to have a circus.

Mrs. Noah did not reply at once. I guess she was thinking it over.

"Well, perhaps they are," she said by and by. "I never thought of it in just that way. I'm afraid I've always thought them mischievous."

"What time shall we have the circus?" asked Ham.

"Not too soon after breakfast," said Capt. Noah. "I don't want any sick animals aboard."

"We'll be careful," said Japheth. "Let's go to bed now so as to wake up bright and early to-morrow."

THE CIRCUS

The ark goes sailing down the bay

Upon the rushing tide;

And the circus will commence to-day

With the animals safe inside.

This is the song the weathercock sang early the next morning.

Marjorie rubbed her eyes, and then jumped out of bed and looked out of the window.

"Good morning," she said to the merry gilt rooster, "it's a fine day for the circus. That was a pretty verse you just sang. Did you make it up?"

"Oh, yes," said the weathercock proudly. "Just couldn't help it, you know. The circus doesn't come to town every day in the week."

Well, after that, Marjorie hurried down to the breakfast table, where she found Mr. Jonah seated with the rest of the family.

She had forgotten all about him, and so had I and maybe you have too, for you see, Mr. Jonah hadn't been feeling very well and had remained in his cabin since the day he'd left the whale.

"It's certainly a relief to be once more at a breakfast table," he said. "Traveling inside a whale is like sailing in a submarine. Although a whale is supposed to be neutral, nevertheless, I was frightened to death for fear we might be torpedoed!"

"Yes, indeed," sighed Mrs. Noah, "these awful times one isn't safe anywhere."

"That's right," exclaimed Capt. Noah, "we must keep a sharp lookout. There's no telling how soon we may be in the war zone, and I am responsible for the safety of all my passengers!"

And just then the Weathercock shouted something which sounded very much like "Periscope!"

Well, you can imagine how excited everybody was after that.

"Where away?" asked Capt. Noah.

"Dead ahead," screamed the Weathercock.

Instantly all eyes were turned in that direction.

Some distance ahead stretched a long, smooth, sandy beach, on which was a huge billboard with the words "Perry's Slope."

"Bah!" exclaimed Capt. Noah, "Perry's Slope isn't 'Periscope.' Well, I'm glad it isn't."

"Are we going ashore?" asked Mr. Jonah.

"Looks like it," answered Capt. Noah; "the ark is pointed for the beach. Hope we don't bump too hard. Some of the animals might get hurt."

The Ark was going at a fast clip, and as they neared the shore every one clung tightly to the railing.

"Hold fast," shouted the Weathercock, as the bow touched the beach.

In another minute the Ark skimmed gracefully over the sand with as much ease as it had sailed upon the ocean.

"Wonderful boat you have," exclaimed Mr. Jonah, looking at Capt. Noah. "Ought to be proud of her. She's a dandy."

Before the latter had time to reply the Ark stopped, and everyone rushed toward the gang-plank. "Let it down easily," commanded Capt. Noah, "easy, there!"

"Why, the Ark's on wheels," cried Marjorie, as she stepped on the sandy beach, "regular automobile wheels."

"Well, I declare," exclaimed Mrs. Noah, "so it is."

"Let's call it the 'Arkmobile,'" suggested Ham.

"Just the thing," said Shem, "don't you think so, father?"

Capt. Noah did not reply for a moment, for he was busily engaged inspecting the bottom of the Ark.

"I was looking to see if it were built to run on the land," he replied, "or whether it just went this far on account of its momentum."

"What's that noise?" asked Japheth.

"Sounds like the engine of an automobile," answered Shem.

"It's coming from the Ark," cried Ham.

Capt. Noah hurriedly went below.

Presently he returned, smiling with satisfaction.

"There's a regular automobile engine in the hold, way aft," he said. "And it's connected with a shaft, so that it will turn the wheels. We'll have no difficulty in traveling on land."

"Hurrah for the Arkmobile!" shouted Ham.

"On land or on sea,

Wherever we be,

The Arkmobile

Is the thing for me,"

sang Marjorie, skipping about on the sand.

"Over sand, over foam,

Wherever we roam,

The Arkmobile

Will carry us home,"

sang the Weathercock, and then he said: "I guess I'll come down from the flagpole if you're going to camp here. If you're not, I'll stay where I am, for it's a pretty good climb, and I'm not much of a sailor as yet."

"Let's stay here and have the circus," said Ham. "We can make a splendid ring in the sand—in fact, we can have three rings if we want to. All we have to do, you know, is to throw up the sand in a circle."

Every one agreed that it was an ideal spot, so the boys set to work at once.

Mrs. Noah made Marjorie a wonderful dress, covered with gold spangles.

"I'm going to ride the big white horse just like a circus rider," cried Marjorie. "And I shall stand up on the saddle and jump through my hoop. Ham can hold it."

"Of course I will," he cried, looking up from his work. "And I'll be jolly glad when this ring is finished. I had no idea it would take so long."

"Hurrah! Mine's finished," cried Japheth.

"And so's mine," shouted Shem.

"Well, I think mine's the biggest of all," said Ham. "It must be, or I'd have finished when you fellows did."

"Father ought to put on his dress suit," said Shem, "and snap the whip when Marjorie rides around the ring. You know just the way they do in the real circus."

"Great Scott!" exclaimed Capt. Noah, overhearing the remark as he descended the gang-plank. "I didn't bargain for this. But I suppose I might as well put it on," and he turned back into the Ark.

The sound of hammering at that moment reached them. "What's going on?" asked Ham.

"Let's see," suggested Shem, but before they reached the gang-plank Mr. Jonah appeared. On his legs were strapped a pair of stilts, which made him at least eight feet high.

"I'm going to be the giant," he said with a laugh, bumping down the gang-plank in a clumsy manner. "I say, Mrs. Noah, could you sew the legs of an old pair of trousers on to mine, so the stilts won't show?"

"Of course I can," replied Mrs. Noah, bursting into laughter. "But I'm afraid they won't match."

In due course of time Marjorie's circus dress was finished and the giant's trousers lengthened, the upper part being blue and the lower part gray, but perfectly satisfactory to the wearer.

Every one was now waiting impatiently for Capt. Noah when, suddenly, his head appeared at one of the port holes. "Mother," he called, "where are my white dress ties? I can't find them anywhere."

So Mrs. Noah laid down her work basket and went into the Ark to find them. And in a few minutes Capt. Noah appeared in full dress, his silk hat upon his head and a long whip in his hand.

As he came down the plank, Japheth led out the big white horse, and after helping Marjorie to mount, led him into the center ring.

Shem then opened the big door in the Ark and all the animals solemnly marched out and arranged themselves about the rings.

Next came Ham, leading his two wrestling monkeys and after him came Shem with his elephant.

Mr. Jonah, towering above the heads of the tallest animals, including the giraffe, announced that the circus would commence.

"Ladies and gentlemen," he began, "allow me to introduce to you the most wonderful child rider in the world, Marjorie Hall, on her beautiful white horse, Marshmallow. Marjorie, without doubt, is the most daring bareback rider in the universe."

There was a great clapping of hands, hoofs and paws at this announcement, for she had become a great favorite with the Noah's Ark people.

"Ladies and gentlemen," went on Mr. Noah, "you see before you in Ring No. 2 the most famous wrestlers of the world, Jocko and Monko. In Ring No. 3 is the largest elephant in existence."

While all this was going on the Noah boys had run into the Ark.

Presently they returned, dressed up as clowns, and then the fun commenced.

Ham held up a hoop, which he had carefully covered with tissue paper, and to Mrs. Noah's amazement Marjorie leaped through it as if she had been a circus bareback rider all her life.

The boys performed marvelous feats of tumbling and jumping, and were so funny that half of the animals nearly split their sides with laughing.

The laughing hyena had to be carried into the Ark and put to bed for fear she would laugh herself to death.

"Well, well," exclaimed Mrs. Noah, when it was all over, "I certainly never enjoyed the circus so much in all my life, not even when I was a little girl."

And that night every one slept like a top, let me tell you, for each one was tired out with the day's work. Even the weathercock, I think, tucked his head under his gilt wings and snored!

THE MAJESTY OF THE LAW

"Wake up! Wake up! We're off again,

Over hill and over plain!

The Arkmobile on sea or land

Can sail away at our command."

Again the Weathercock awoke little Marjorie, on board the Noah's Ark, where we left her in the last chapter, you remember.

It was the morning after the circus, and she probably would have slept much later had not the faithful bird, as usual, sung his bit of verse.

You see this wonderful Weathercock was just like an alarm clock.

"Where's the ocean?" asked Marjorie, looking out of the window. "Why, we're traveling on land!"

"Of course we are," answered the Weathercock. "Didn't you see the wheels on the bottom of the Ark yesterday?"

"So I did," admitted Marjorie. "I'd forgotten all about them."

"Well, how did you like my poetry? You see, I make up a new verse every morning, so as to be sure to wake you up."

"I think you are a great poet," answered the little girl.

The Weathercock got very red in the gills. I guess that's the only way he could blush.

So let the rain or sunshine come,

Across the land, we'll swiftly hum,

We are prepared for rain or shine,

For dusty road or foamy brine.

"Hurrah!" shouted the Elephant from down below. "Bravo, Sir Chanticleer!"

"You'll have to excuse me now," said Marjorie to the Weathercock, "for I must pull on my shoes and stockings and brush my hair. You don't have to bother about such things, you know. That's one advantage of being a weathercock."

After breakfast, as they all sat in the cabin, Capt. Noah remarked: "I'm getting a trifle worried. You see, I can't tell by the barometer whether the Ark is floating or wheeling. Now, that is rather important. If we keep on in this way I shall have to get a speedometer. It wouldn't be very nice to be arrested for breaking the speed laws and be locked up in jail."

Mrs. Noah turned pale and the Weathercock shifted about uneasily on the top of the flagpole. "No, indeed," he said, "I don't want to be a jailbird."

"Well, what's the best thing to do?" asked Mrs. Noah.

"Count the telegraph poles as we go along," suggested Ham. "I think there are about thirty to a mile, and see how long it takes to pass them."

"That's a good idea," said Mr. Jonah, but when they looked out of the portholes they couldn't find any telegraph poles.

And just then, all of a sudden, a pistol shot rang out clear and loud.

The Arkmobile came to a sudden stop, and a voice outside was heard to exclaim:

"Where's the chauffeur?"

Capt. Noah rushed up on deck, followed by his family, Mr. Jonah and Marjorie.

"What's the matter?" asked Capt. Noah, looking about to find the owner of the voice.

"Oh, that's what they all say!" came the reply. "You know jolly well what's the matter!"

"Who are you, and where are you?" asked Capt. Noah, vainly trying to find this remarkable person, who seemed to be nothing but a voice.

"Who am I? You'll find out pretty quick. Where am I? You'd better find that out even quicker!"

Looking up to the Weathercock, Capt. Noah shouted: "Ahoy, there, Lookout! Who's delaying us?"

"The Majesty of the Law," came the answering voice again—this time so distinctly that every one turned in the direction from which it came, and then a huge megaphone on the top of a post repeated: "The Majesty of the Law!"

"Well, I'll be blowed!" exclaimed Capt. Noah.

"You have exceeded the speed limit," said the Megaphone, "and you are fined $15!"

"Oh!" interposed Mrs. Noah. "I'm sure you must be mistaken. I'm sure we were not exceeding it $15 worth."

"So am I!" added Mr. Jonah. "In fact, I didn't think we were exceeding anything. We were just rolling along, don't you know, quite comfortably."

"Well, suppose I haven't the money with me?" asked Capt. Noah.

"Fifteen days in jail," answered the Megaphone.

"Mercy!" cried Mrs. Noah.

"Don't worry," whispered Capt. Noah. "I'll borrow the money from Mr. Jonah."

Mr. Jonah was very obliging and lent the money, saying he had had no chance to spend a cent while he was aboard the whale.

"Now, where shall I put the money?" asked Capt. Noah.

"In the little box back of me," replied the Megaphone. And as soon as the money was dropped in the Megaphone shouted: "The prisoner is discharged!"

"Prisoner!" shouted Capt. Noah, as mad as a hornet. "How dare you call me a prisoner!"

But before he had time to say another word the Arkmobile started off and the Megaphone was left behind.

"Jehosaphat!" exclaimed Capt. Noah, wiping the perspiration from his forehead with his red bordered handkerchief. "Bad enough to be robbed of $15, but to be called a 'prisoner'—well, that does make me angry."

"Never mind, my dear," said Mrs. Noah, soothingly. "All's well that ends well. Just think, if we hadn't been able to borrow that $15, we'd have spent fifteen days in jail!"

And then, all of a sudden the Weathercock shouted: "Everybody in the cabin! Water dead ahead!"

My goodness me! you should have seen the animals pull their heads in through the portholes. Poor Mrs. Giraffe didn't get hers inside in time and her bonnet got soaking wet, for as soon as the Ark struck the water the spray flew here and there and everywhere and the deck was flooded ankle deep.

But the Ark was a sturdy craft, and as soon as it once more felt the ocean beneath it, rode the waves as gracefully as a swan.

"I guess we won't be fined for speeding now," laughed Marjorie, and in the next chapter you shall hear what further adventures she had aboard this wonderful Noah's Ark.

MAN OVERBOARD

Wake up! Wake up! and sing your song

As we roll merrily along.

Above the meadow sings the lark,

So let us sing aboard the Ark.

"There goes the Weathercock," cooed the Dove, flying over to the porthole
and looking out over the bright blue ocean.

"Tell him I'll get up in a minute," yawned Marjorie.

So the Dove, who slept in Marjorie's cabin in a pretty gilt cage, spoke to the
Weathercock, after which she commenced to sing:

There's a robin in the woodland,

There's a robin in the sea,

But they are just as different

As different can be.

The one that's in the forest

Has feathers and a tail;

The one that's in the ocean

Has a scaly coat of mail.

The robin in the forest

Could never take a swim;

The robin of the ocean

Could never fly or skim

Across a grassy meadow,

Nor fly up in a tree.

But he can do all kinds of stunts

Within the deep blue sea.

"Where did you learn all that?" asked Marjorie, pulling on her stockings.

"Listen; there's another verse and maybe two or three," cooed the Dove, and then she began to sing again:

The robin of the woodland

Has a pretty crimson vest;

He sings a merry, blithesome song

And builds a cozy nest.

The robin of the ocean

Has fins that look like wings.

He doesn't build a nest at all,

He grunts, but never sings.

Yet both of them are robins,

As some of us have heard —

Although the ocean one's a fish,

The woodland one's a bird.

"Cock-a-doodle-do!" crowed the Weathercock, as the Dove finished her song.

"Hurrah for you! You are the poet of the Ark."

"Oh, no!" replied the modest little Dove. "That is not my own. My mother taught me that song when I was a Dovelet."

"Is that so?" said the Weathercock, and he gave a sigh of relief, for I guess he wanted to be the only poet on board the Ark and sing his little songs every morning just as he had always done.

By this time Marjorie was dressed and, taking the Dove on her shoulder, went down to the diningroom. As usual, the Noah boys were on hand with great and glorious appetites.

"How are the animals this morning?" inquired Capt. Noah, helping himself to a big saucer of oatmeal.

"Pretty well," answered Japheth.

"Some of the insects are getting restless," said Ham.

"I should say so," exclaimed Mrs. Noah. "Here's that big red Ant in the sugar bowl."

"Catch him," cried Shem, "we ought to put him back where he belongs."'

But the Ant all of a sudden crawled out of the sugar bowl and ran down the leg of the table and out on deck.

"There he goes!" shouted Marjorie.

"Quick, or he'll get away!" cried Capt. Noah. "I can't afford to lose a single passenger!" Instantly the boys darted after the fleeing insect, but just as they were about to snatch him up from the deck a wave washed him overboard.

"Man overboard!" shouted the Weathercock.

And, my goodness! What a commotion there was after that! All the animals rushed up on deck to see who had fallen into the ocean.

"Throw him a life-preserver!" yelled Mr. Jonah, and in a second Ham unfastened a large "horsecollar" life-preserver and tossed it into the ocean.

"Suppose he can't reach it," said the elephant. "I guess I'd better jump in and save him," and overboard went the big animal with a loud splash.

"Where is he?" asked the Elephant, after looking around in vain for the Ant. "I can't see him!"

And no wonder, for the sea was rough, and it was no easy matter to find so small a passenger.

"Get my telescope!" yelled Capt. Noah.

"I think it's in my workbasket," said Mrs. Noah to Ham, who started at once to obey his father's command. "If it isn't it may be in your toolchest. I think you had it the other day when you were going to make an anti-aircraft gun out of it for your toy army."

"That's where I found it," said Ham, a minute later, appearing breathless with the telescope.

"Where abouts?" screamed the Elephant, who was now some distance from the Ark.

"Wait a minute, can't you?" yelled Capt. Noah. "I've got to adjust the thing. These boys have been meddling with it!"

When this was finally done, Capt. Noah swept the sea with his glass, but in vain; the form of the poor Ant was nowhere to be seen.

"Shiver my timbers!" said Capt. Noah, under his breath. "What will happen to me if I lose a passenger?"

"Hurry up!" gasped the Elephant, now thoroughly worn out by the buffeting of the waves. "Hurry up, I'm most in."

"Well, we'll have to get you out, then," answered Capt. Noah.

"Swim around to the port side," said Ham; "we'll hoist you up by the davits."

"I hate to give up looking for the Ant," said the Elephant, as he slipped the ropes under his big body.

And then, after much tugging and hauling away on the ropes he was lifted up even with the deck. But beyond this it was impossible to do anything. The davits refused to swing in, being hindered by the immense size of the animal.

"Put your trunk on the deck," suggested Mr. Jonah. "That will make you weigh less, and perhaps we can roll you over the edge."

"Yes, that's a good idea," said Shem. "Put your baggage aboard first."

"This is no time for joking——We have lost one passenger and are in danger of losing another. It will look very strange to lose the largest and the smallest on the same day," said poor Capt. Noah, despairingly.

Well, just then, Mrs. Elephant came up from the hold. She had overslept herself, and had only now heard the commotion on deck. On seeing her mate swinging from the davits she set up a loud trumpeting.

"Goodness, gracious, Ella!" said the Elephant. "Don't carry on like that. Screaming won't get me out. Get hold of me and help pull."

This was good advice, and pretty soon Mr. Elephant was landed safely on board the Ark.

Just then the Weathercock called out that he could see the little red Ant on the life-preserver.

"Thank goodness!" exclaimed Capt. Noah, and the Ark was turned in the direction pointed out by the faithful lookout. Then Mr. Jonah leaned over and pulled in the life-preserver as the Ark slowly came alongside, and just in the nick of time, for the poor Ant was nearly dead.

"Give him to me," said Mrs. Noah. "A little Jamaica ginger and a warm blanket will bring him 'round, I guess."

"Well, well!" exclaimed Capt. Noah, as the motherly form of Mrs. Noah disappeared down the companionway. "This has been an exciting forenoon," and then he wiped his forehead with his red bordered handkerchief and looked about him. "All you animals go below deck!" he commanded, "or else we'll have somebody else overboard."

So Mrs. Elephant led Mr. Elephant, who was wet to the skin and shivering with the cold, down to the hold, where she put him to bed with a hot water bag at his feet and a woolen night cap on his head.

"Are you going to put this down in your log book?" asked Marjorie. "I think it will make a very interesting story and I've heard from old sailors that they always put down everything that happens in the log book."

"Of course I will," answered Capt. Noah. "Bring me the log book, Japheth. You haven't done anything this morning. Suppose you jot it down. I declare, I'm all tuckered out with excitement and worry."

"You'd better lie down and rest, father," said Mrs. Noah, coming up on deck. "I have the Ant very comfortable now, and I feel sure he will recover in a short time."

So Capt. Noah went below to rest, and the little Dove perched herself on Marjorie's shoulder and watched Capt. Noah's son write in the log book.

And what do you suppose he wrote? Well, it was something like this, for the little Dove told me afterwards:

The little red Ant fell into the sea,

But, oh, dear you, and oh, dear me!

And then the Elephant with a shout

Jumped in and tried to pull him out.

But he wasn't saved by the Elephant;

It was Mr. Jonah who saved the Ant.

And in the next chapter I'll tell you more about Marjorie on board the Ark.

FIRE! FIRE!

"Fire! Fire! Fire!"

Marjorie awoke with a start. The Weathercock was again sounding the warning, "Fire! Fire! Fire!"

"Where?" cried Marjorie, looking out of the porthole at the excited Weathercock and then down to the deck, where at that moment Capt. Noah and his sons appeared, each armed with a pail.

The fire evidently was at the forward end of the Ark, for Noah and his crew ran in that direction.

It took Marjorie but a few minutes to dress, and just as she reached the deck, Mr. Jonah appeared.

"This is a poor way to put out a fire," he said, as he tossed the water from his pail down the hatchway, from which was rising a thick cloud of smoke. "We need a hose and a pump."

"Hurry up, Jonah!" commanded Capt. Noah. "This fire is getting too much headway to suit me. I'm afraid the animals will be roasted if we don't put it out pretty soon!"

As he finished speaking the Elephant rushed on deck and, leaning over the side of the Ark, filled his trunk with water, which he immediately squirted over himself. And then Mrs. Elephant did the same.

"I was never so warm before," she remarked; "not even in India. If I had stayed another minute below deck I would have been scarred for life!"

By this time the deck was crowded. Some of the animals were nearly frightened to death; some were choking with the smoke, while others were filling the air with noises of all kinds. It was as if pandemonium were let loose.

Those animals which could climb were soon scrambling to the roof of the Ark, where they sat on or clung desperately to the ridgepole.

The deck grew hotter and hotter, and it was necessary for every one to dance about in order to keep his feet from blistering.

"Holy sufferin' mackerel!" exclaimed Capt. Noah, now realizing the seriousness of the situation. "Are we to be burned at sea?"

"Get the Elephants to squirt water down the hold," suggested Ham.

"Get busy," said Capt. Noah to the Elephants. "Your trunks are nearly as good as hose. Why don't you help us?"

"What do you say, Ella?" said the Elephant. "If we don't we may have to swim later."

Without answering, she went forward and commenced drawing up the salt water in her trunk and then sending it in a swift stream down into the hold. The fire, however, was gaining fast, and in spite of the efforts of the Elephants and the crew the danger increased to an alarming extent, and at last the flames leaped forth and crawled over the deck.

The animals howled and rushed to the stern of the Ark, which raised the bow high in the air, and thus added to the danger.

"If it would only rain!" said Mrs. Noah, who sat on a coil of rope, her sealskin coat on her arm and her jewel box in her hand.

"If it would only rain! This can't be the forty-first day, can it? Time does go so fast."

Well, I guess something terrible would have happened if just then all of a sudden the Weathercock hadn't seen the Whale, who had landed Mr. Jonah aboard, some two or three chapters ago.

"There's the Whale!" shouted the Weathercock. "See him spout!"

"Run up a signal of distress!" commanded Capt. Noah. "He might save Mr. Jonah for old times' sake!"

"If he'd only get up close and spout water over the Ark, he'd put out the fire pretty quick," said Ham.

"Good idea," said Capt. Noah. "Ship ahoy!" yelled Mr. Jonah, waving his red bandanna handkerchief in the air. "Ahoy! Ahoy!"

Then the Whale stopped spouting and made for the Ark.

"He's coming! He's coming!" shouted the Weathercock.

"Don't stop squirting water," said Capt. Noah to the Elephants.

"On with the pail brigade!" screamed Ham. And then the monkeys slid down from the roof and grabbed hold of the pails and threw water down the hold. But still the cruel flames crept nearer and nearer.

"Oh, dear!" sighed Mrs. Noah. "I'm afraid my sealskin coat will get singed, and after all the trouble I've had putting it up in camphor."

And then, all of a sudden, a tremendous stream of water fell upon the Ark, soaking every one to the skin. And soon the deck was a river, and the steam that came out of the hold almost suffocated everybody.

"Goodness me!" screamed Mrs. Noah. "We'll be swamped!"

"Hold on, there," shouted Capt. Noah, leaning over the side of the Ark, where the Whale lay like a fire patrol boat in action. "Hold on! Turn off the hose, or you'll drown us!"

So the good-natured Whale shut off the water, while Capt. Noah added: "A Turkish bath has nothing on this!"

"It was awfully kind of you to come to our rescue," said Mrs. Noah, smiling sweetly at the Whale as she leaned over the railing.

"Well, if you hadn't come just when you did," said Capt. Noah, "I guess we'd all have gone down to Davey Jones' locker."

"Don't mention it," said the Whale. "Glad to have been able to do you a little favor. You see," he added in a low voice, "Mr. Jonah was never satisfied when he was my guest. He was always complaining about the dampness. So when you came along and I had a chance to put him aboard the Ark I was tickled to death. In fact, I was so glad to get rid of my passenger that I made up this little poem," and then the Whale began to spout:

"It's not so very pleasant, when sailing on the sea,

To have a passenger aboard who's sulky as can be;

And that's the reason, after dark,

I landed him aboard the Ark."

And after that he swam away, and the Ark began once more to skim over the dark blue sea. And by and by, after a while, Capt. Noah said:

"We'll have to make new bunks and berths for the animals, I guess, for the fire has burned up everything."

And, oh, dear me! When he went below he saw that everything was burned to a cinder.

"We'll have to land somewhere and make repairs," said Mr. Jonah.

"I guess we will," said Capt. Noah, and all the animals began to howl and make dreadful noises, for they didn't want to go down in the smoky hold, you see.

And just then all of a sudden the Weathercock called out:

"Land to starboard!"

And, sure enough, looming up in the dim distance was a mountainous shore line.

REPAIRS

Ahoy, ahoy, Mount Ararat,

Now we know where we are at.

Run the Ark up high and dry,

Close against the bright blue sky.

"Not a bit of it!" shouted Capt. Noah, looking up at the Weathercock, "I don't propose to take any chances running up that mountain side. Suppose our motor gave out? We'd be in a nice fix. We'll run up on the shore and heave to."

The Ark, obeying Capt. Noah's guiding hand, swept up on the beach and came to a standstill some 200 feet from the water.

"We can cut all the timber we need for repairs now," said Japheth, looking over toward a big forest that lay back from the beach. "The animals, too, can have a nice frolic on the sand. It will do them good after being cooped up on board ship for so long."

And in a short time the Ark was empty and all the animals were having a fine time making castles in the sand and picking up pretty sea shells.

And after a while Capt. Noah got out his axe and saw, and calling to Mr. Jonah, and his three boys, started off for the forest, and as soon as he cut down a tree, Mr. Jonah and the three boys sawed it up into logs.

"I guess we have enough now," said Capt. Noah. "Guess we'd better start and split them into planks."

This was not such easy work, but after a while, they had quite a pile of lumber on hand.

"If we only had a wagon to haul the logs to the Ark," said Capt. Noah, wiping his forehead with his red bordered handkerchief.

And just then Marjorie came riding down the gang-plank in the little toy automobile.

"I'll take them back to the Ark," she said, and after a while, not so very long, they were all aboard.

Well, by this time it was pretty dark, and Capt. Noah felt uneasy about the animals, so he stood up on the bow of the big boat and called out:

"All aboard for the night!"

"All aboard for the night!" he called out again, and then he turned to little Marjorie and said, "I'd never forgive myself if anything should happen to any one of my passengers."

But, oh dear me! When Capt. Noah, who had stood by the gang-plank and checked off each animal as he came aboard, found that the little red squirrel was missing, he was dreadfully worried.

"Goodness me!" he exclaimed, "if that squirrel has gone off into the woods, how will we ever find him?"

"Well, there's no use in worrying," said Mrs. Noah, who just then came up from below deck. "Come down and get a nice hot cup of tea. After you've eaten something you'll know better what to do."

Well, after supper, everybody felt better, so Capt. Noah and his crew came up on deck to look for the lost squirrel.

The moon was just coming up out of the east, making a silver path across the water right up to the Ark.

As Capt. Noah looked over the railing to the sand below he saw a little figure walking directly in the silver moon path. It seemed to be carrying something heavy; for it paused every now and then to rest.

"It's the little red squirrel," shouted Marjorie.

"So it is," said Capt. Noah.

"Helloa, there!" he shouted, "wait and I'll let down the gang-plank!"

"Whew, but I'm tired!" panted the red squirrel, as he crawled up on deck. "This bag of nuts is as heavy as lead!"

And then he let the well-filled bag slip from his shoulders to the deck.

"Don't you ever stay out as late as this again, sir," said Capt. Noah, pulling in the gang-plank and making it fast for the night. "If you do, you won't get shore leave for a long time."

"I'm glad you're back," whispered Marjorie, "for we were all dreadfully worried about you," and this so pleased the little red squirrel that he gave her a handful of chestnuts.

"Come along with me," said Capt. Noah, "I'm going below to see what the boys are doing."

So Marjorie and the little squirrel followed the captain without a word, for they saw that he was somewhat vexed.

Below deck all was in confusion, for the animals, after finishing their supper, were trying to find places to sleep.

Although Mr. Jonah and the boys had made the place as clean as possible since the fire, they had not, of course, been able in so short a time to replace the bunks and pens in which the animals had slept.

Everybody was in everybody else's way.

The smaller animals were squeezed into corners by the larger ones, and the Elephant complained that the red Ant kept treading on his toes.

"Order! Order!" shouted Capt. Noah.

"What are you doing, Jonah, and where are you, boys?" he called out, peering into the darkness, for of course all the electric lights were out and the hold was in total darkness.

"Here we are," answered Mr. Jonah. "We're doing the best we can," and he came out of the darkness and rested his pitchfork on the floor while he wiped the perspiration from his forehead.

"I was spreading out the straw for bedding. Ham is giving the pigs a drink before they go to bed."

And just then the other two boys appeared. "What are you doing here?" Japheth asked the muley cow, which stood by quietly chewing her cud.

But the muley cow only said, "Moo-o-oo!"

"Well, you come along with me. All the cows are at the other end of the Ark."

"Don't be impatient," said Capt. Noah, for the muley cow was a very gentle creature and never tried to butt any one with her horns, because she didn't have any, you know.

While all this was going on Marjorie and the little squirrel stood in the doorway.

"Glad you weren't lost," said Shem, patting the squirrel on the back as if he were a little pet dog. "The other squirrels said they wouldn't go to bed until you were found."

"Where are they?" asked the little red squirrel. "I'm pretty sleepy and would like to cuddle up for the night," and then he swung his bag of nuts over his shoulder and followed Shem, but before he went he whispered to Marjorie that he'd give her some hickory nuts in the morning.

After a while everything was made snug and tight for the night. Mr. Jonah put away his pitchfork and the boys hung up the water pails. Then a lighted lantern was hung at each end of the cabin, and the evening chores were done, just the same as if they had been on a farm, you know.

And after that Marjorie went up on deck, where the weathercock was sitting on the flagpole in the moonlight.

"Oh, I love to be a sailor

And sail the ocean blue,

And hear the Captain shout 'Ahoy!'

And order 'round the crew.

"And when the waves are rolling high

The wind is blowing strong,

I sing my cock-a-doodle-do

Just like a sailor song.

"Oh, I'm a sailor rooster,

And my name is Shanghai Joe,

And I'll sail the sea from A to Z,

I'm a sailor bird, Heave ho!"

"Well, I'm glad you're so happy," said little Marjorie, and maybe she felt just a little bit homesick, for she was far away from home. And just then Mrs. Noah came on deck and said, "Come, Madge, it's time for bed," and then she picked her up and carried her into her cabin and tucked her in for the night as comfortable as you please. And in the next chapter I'll tell you what happened in the morning.

THE ICEBERG

Jingle bells! Jingle bells!
It's getting cold as ice,
Put your furs and mittens on,
Wrap up warm and nice.

Marjorie awoke with a start. My, how cold it was! The porthole glass was covered with a network of frosty lace, and the little Dove, who slept in Marjorie's cabin, pulled her head out from under her wing and shivered.

"What has happened?" asked Marjorie, sitting up in bed and looking about her.

Perhaps she expected to see Jack Frost sitting in the rocking chair!

Quickly pulling on her slippers she ran to the porthole to ask her good friend the Weathercock the reason for this sudden drop in the temperature. She found him, as usual, perched on the flagpole. His comb was very red, as if Jack Frost had given it a nip, and now and then he raised one leg to his breast to warm his toes in the fluffy feathers.

"Good morning," said Marjorie. "Isn't it freezing?"

"Do you wonder?" answered the Weathercock, pointing to a large iceberg close at hand.

She turned to look and, sure enough, just a few feet away was a great mountain of ice.

"We're aground on an iceberg," went on the Weathercock. "We ran into an ice floe last night and the Ark slipped upon the ledge of the iceberg and grounded."

"Goodness gracious!" cried Marjorie. "What are we ever going to do?"

"I'm sure I don't know," answered the Weathercock. "I'll have to get some woolen socks and a pair of felt shoes or my toes will be frostbitten!"

"Perhaps Mrs. Noah will knit you a pair," said Marjorie. "I'm going down to breakfast now and I'll speak to her about it."

"Thank you," replied the Weathercock. "And tell her I wouldn't mind having a worsted muffler, too."

Down below matters were even worse, for the fresh water had frozen during the night, so that it was impossible to give the animals a drink.

Mrs. Noah had been forced to melt a piece of ice in a pan over the fire in order to have water with which to make the coffee.

"Whew!" exclaimed Capt. Noah, coming in from deck and closing the door as quickly as possible. "My hands are almost frozen. This is as bad as a trip to the North Pole. Perhaps worse, for we are totally unprepared for this kind of weather."

Just then Mr. Jonah and the boys came in, rubbing their hands and stamping their feet to keep warm.

"Merry Christmas!" laughed Ham, "the skating's fine out on the ice floe!"

"How jolly!" cried Marjorie. "Let's go skating after breakfast!"

"No, sir-e-e," said Capt. Noah. "The boys must help me float the Ark. One of the rubber-tired wheels is crushed and it will take a lot of hard work to get her off."

"We'd better set about it as soon as possible," said Mr. Jonah, after Capt. Noah had made an inspection. "Some of the animals are nearly perishing with the cold. The monkeys are rolled up so tight you'd think they were fur balls. Only the polar bears seem to enjoy life, and they are just crazy to take a run on the ice."

"Let them wait," said Capt. Noah; "we have more serious things to attend to than pleasure for the moment."

"Well, come and get a good hot breakfast first," said Mrs. Noah, bringing in the steaming coffee pot and a plate of hot corn muffins. "After breakfast you'll all feel differently."

This was, indeed, good advice, and when breakfast was over Capt. Noah said, "Get the crowbar and the wooden rollers, Japheth. We'll see if we can't start the old Ark moving. Maybe she's stuck too deep in the ice, but we'll try, at any rate."

"Here, my little girl," said kind Mrs. Noah to Marjorie, "put on this muffler if you're going out. It's pretty cold."

So Marjorie tied the warm muffler around her neck and stepped out on deck.

A beautiful sight met her eyes. Towering high above was a mountain of glittering ice, while as far as the eye could reach was a field of ice and snow.

Under the rays of the morning sun parts of the great berg glittered like a rainbow.

It was so cold that Marjorie had to jump up and down to keep her toes from freezing.

Down on the ice, close to the Ark, Capt. Noah and his crew were busily at work. One of the auto wheels had sunk deep into the ice and acted like an anchor. The other wheels also were embedded in the ice so that the Ark was held as if in a vise.

"Guess we'll have to give it up," exclaimed Capt. Noah after an hour's hard work, during which time the Ark had not moved an inch.

"We'd better make up our minds to winter here until the iceberg floats into a warmer climate and either melts or breaks apart."

"That's cheerful," said Mr. Jonah. "I've nothing but summer flannels and a mackintosh with me."

"What about some of the poor animals who are used to the Torrid Zone?" replied Capt. Noah, shouldering the crowbar and climbing up the rope ladder to the deck.

Mr. Jonah did not reply, but turned up his coat collar and stamped upon his feet to warm them.

"The hairless Mexican dog will surely die if we don't do something for him," said Ham. "I think I'll ask mother if she won't let him stay in the kitchen."

But Mrs. Noah did not seem very pleased over the suggestion.

"Gracious me!" she said. "Shem already has two parrots, a marmoset and a little green snake in the kitchen. I don't suppose one more animal would make much difference, if it will only keep from under my feet. I nearly stepped on one of the snakes this morning, and the kitchen is none too large, anyway."

"Don't you boys worry your mother any more," said Capt. Noah sternly. "The animals have got to make the best of it. Any one who travels by sea undergoes some risk and I'm sure I'm as careful a captain as a man could be. It's lucky we didn't go down to the bottom of the sea when we struck the berg, instead of running up on it safely."

After dinner Capt. Noah and Mr. Jonah held a consultation as to what was the best thing to do under the circumstances.

"Of course, some of the animals, like the polar bears and the seals, will enjoy a vacation on the ice. The penguins, too, will be glad to have a little change. We can let them out and the rest of the Arctic passengers. But how to keep the other animals warm, puzzles me. We haven't coal enough to keep the furnaces going for very long."

Mr. Jonah stroked his chin reflectively. "We might dig a channel from the Ark to the edge of the berg and then float the Ark," he said, after a pause.

"That's a pretty good scheme," said Capt. Noah. "We'll get to work at once. Here, you boys, get the pickaxes and come with me."

By evening the canal was finished. "Now, when the tide rises," said Capt. Noah, resting on the handle of his pickax, "perhaps the old tub will float."

It was now quite dark, so all hands returned to the Ark.

The animals which had been allowed to play on the ice had all returned except the two polar bears, who begged Capt. Noah to let them stay out all night, as they wished to see the Northern Lights from the top of the iceberg.

It was a very tired family that gathered around the supper table that evening. But after the meal was over the Weathercock began to sing:

"It's time for bed, and all the Ark
Should soon be snoring in the dark,

The elephant and kangaroo,

The lion and the curled horn gnu,

Have gone to bed, and so should you,

So good night, cock-a-doodle-doo!"

A THRILLING RESCUE

We're off! we're off! we're off again

To sail upon the rolling main.

The ice no longer holds us fast,

We're sailing safe and free at last!

This is what the Weathercock sang loud and clear the next morning.

It woke up Marjorie with a start, and running to the porthole she saw that they were once more upon the ocean blue.

"How did it happen?" she asked, turning to her faithful friend on the flagpole, who was still crowing and flapping his wings at a great rate. "How did it all happen?"

"While you were asleep, my dear little Madge," answered the Weathercock.

"I didn't ask you when, I asked you how," laughed Marjorie, for she was delighted, you see, to be once more sailing over the great big ocean.

"You'd better not ask me any more questions," said the Weathercock quickly. "You just better hurry up and dress and ask Capt. Noah what he is going to do about the castaways."

"The what?" gasped Marjorie.

"The castaways. The two polar bears who are still on the iceberg."

"Goodness gracious!" she cried. "I'll hurry and get on my boots. I must tell Capt. Noah at once."

In a few minutes she was running down to the lower cabin.

"Capt. Noah! Capt. Noah!" she shouted. "Capt. Noah, the polar bears are left on the iceberg!"

The captain, who had overslept himself, put his head out of his cabin door.

"What is all the excitement about?" he asked sleepily.

"The bears are left on the iceberg!" shouted Marjorie again.

"Well, that's all right. I told them they could stay out all night. They will come aboard for breakfast, no doubt!"

"They can't! They can't!" cried Marjorie in great excitement. "The Ark is afloat again and we are sailing away."

"Blubber and rubber!" exclaimed the captain, now even more excited than the little girl.

"Mother!" he cried, "the Ark's afloat and two of our passengers are still ashore!"

Mrs. Noah opened her eyes.

"What did you say, my dear?" she asked, sleepily.

The captain by this time had pulled on his sailor suit and, closing the cabin door with a bang, rushed out on deck, with Marjorie close at his heels.

In the distance the iceberg could be seen indistinctly through the morning mist.

"Hard-a-port!" shouted Capt. Noah.

Mr. Jonah, who was at the wheel, woke up with a start. He was so tired with cutting the ice the day before that he had fallen sound asleep at his post.

"You landlubber," cried Capt. Noah. "What do you mean by falling asleep?"

"This is my first experience before the mast," apologized poor Jonah. "I've always been a passenger. Please don't get provoked."

"Provoked!" yelled Capt. Noah. "Provoked! I feel like throwing you overboard!"

"Steer for the iceberg!"

"I won't throw you overboard until later!"

Mr. Jonah heaved a sigh of relief, for at first I guess he thought he'd have to go back to the Whale without having the chance of Capt. Noah cooling off.

Marjorie stood close to the rail, straining her eyes for a glimpse of the polar bears.

The three Noah boys now came on deck, and Ham handed the spyglass to his father.

"I see them! I see them!" cried Capt. Noah. "One of them is waving a flag!"

"Let me look," said Marjorie, who was dreadfully worried about them.

Yes, there they were. On the top of the berg she could dimly see two figures and a white object waving back and forth. The sea was getting rough and the Ark rolled about in a most uncomfortable manner.

The Weathercock clung tightly to his post, however, and flapped his wings now and then.

"Look out!" he cautioned as the Ark neared the berg. "Be careful or you'll stave a hole in the Ark!"

"Hurry up!" shouted the polar bears. "We're nearly starved. We want our breakfast."

"Want your breakfast!" muttered Capt. Noah under his breath. "You'll be wanting something more than breakfast if we don't find a way to get you aboard!"

"Let them swim!" suggested Ham.

"Run up close and let them jump!" advised Shem.

"Let them fly!" chuckled Japheth, unsympathetically, who was somewhat tired of feeding the animals and felt that two less would not be such an awful thing after all.

"Nothing of the sort," cried Capt. Noah. "I am responsible for the safety of every passenger. I will take no such chances."

"What are we going to do, then?" asked Mr. Jonah, looking over the side of the Ark to make sure that it was not getting too close to the dangerous berg, which jutted out in ragged points beneath the water.

"Launch the life-boat!" commanded Capt. Noah. "Who will volunteer?"

"I will!" cried Ham, and in less time than I can take to tell it, Ham and his trained monkeys lowered the boat and jumped in.

"Shove off!" commanded Cockswain Ham, and with a strong pull and a loud "Yo-ho!" the little boat shot away.

Ham held firmly to the tiller and kept the bow pointed toward the big rollers, while the monkeys handled the oars.

"Pull for the shore, sailor, pull for the shore," sang the Weathercock.

The bears, who had slid down the iceberg close to the water's edge, stood anxiously waiting.

"Careful, now!" cried Ham. "Pull on your starboard oar!"

The boat grazed the iceberg. "Jump!" shouted Ham. "Quick!"

And then one of the bears gave a spring and landed in the boat. His mate, however, slipped, and a big wave at that moment whirled the boat away from the ice, and with a big splash he landed in the water.

"Throw him a life-preserver!" shouted Capt. Noah.

"Throw him a life line!" yelled Shem.

"Throw him the anchor!" growled Japheth, who never had liked the Polar Bears, I guess.

But Cockswain Ham was not the least bit rattled. He steered the boat toward the frightened bear and told him to catch hold.

"Now pull for all you're worth!" shouted Ham to the monkeys, "and we'll tow Brother Bear."

But, oh, dear me! The great waves kept washing over the little boat, and the two monkeys had a hard time rowing with that great heavy bear dragging on the stern.

"They'll be swamped!" screamed Mrs. Noah, as a tremendous great wave dashed over the little life-boat.

"Bail, bail, you lubber!" shouted Ham. "We'll all be in Davy Jones's locker if you don't!"

Well, pretty soon they came alongside the Ark, and Capt. Noah let down a rope ladder, up which the two bears managed to scramble after a hard struggle.

And after that Cockswain Ham and his gallant crew came aboard, and the life-boat was hoisted up on deck.

Motherly Mrs. Noah at once put the two bears to bed after a hot mustard bath and a drink of Jamaica ginger.

"Well, this beats the old days all holler!" exclaimed Capt. Noah. "We never had such accidents on my first voyage. It just rained and rained for forty days and forty nights."

"That's the truth, my dear," agreed Mrs. Noah. "I remember it very well. Ham was just a baby, and the other two boys were little fellows. It was hard work finding something new for them to do each day. Rainy days on board ship—well, I never want to go through with it again."

"I should think your boys would think you're just lovely," said little Marjorie.

"Well, I guess we do," said Ham, kissing his mother. "You know we do, mother dear."

"Of course I do," she replied, giving him a hug.

"Go and kiss your mother," said Capt. Noah to Shem and Japheth, "or she won't give you any breakfast."

And then they both ran over to her and kissed her, glad of an excuse to show their real feelings.

"Now, come and get something nice and hot for breakfast," said Mrs. Noah, "for if we don't eat breakfast pretty soon, we'll have to call it lunch."

And in the next chapter you shall hear of a dreadful collision, but don't worry, for I shan't let anything happen to little Marjorie and the kind Noah family.

A LEAK

"Look out! Look out! A boat in sight;

Turn quickly to the left or right;

You'll have a smash-up, sure as fate —

Alas! my warning came too late!"

sang the Weathercock.

And, oh, dear me! He was right! Crash! Bang! The Noah's Ark shivered from bow to stern, and all the animals were thrown off their feet.

Little Marjorie awoke with a start. It was just daylight, and far off in the east the rising sun was tinging the sky pink and gold.

She hurriedly put on her clothes and ran out on deck, where she met Capt. Noah and his sons.

"Whales and porpoises!" exclaimed Capt. Noah. "Mr. Jonah has been asleep at the switch again, I'll bet!"

And then he ran forward and looked over the bow of the Ark.

Only a few yards off was the charred hull of a vessel, riding low in the water.

Quickly examining his own ship, Capt. Noah discovered a hole on the starboard side.

And then, all of a sudden, the animals came rushing up on deck.

"The Ark is filling with water," cried Mrs. Elephant, "and my slippers are all soaking wet. If I had remained below another minute they would have been ruined!"

She had hardly finished when all the rats and mice scrambled up the companionway.

"A bad sign!" said Capt. Noah. "It shows the Ark is sinking!"

Mrs. Noah gave a scream. She had hastily thrown a kimono over her nightdress at the first warning and had hurried on deck.

"Don't worry," said little Marjorie bravely. "Capt. Noah will stop the leak."

"I hope so," he said. Then, turning to the passengers, he asked: "Who will volunteer to go with me below deck?"

"I will!" shouted Ham.

"And so will I!" said the Elephant.

"Come along, then," said Capt. Noah.

"Throw me down the tarpaulin and some planks," he called up a few minutes later.

But, oh dear me! The water had gained such headway that the tarpaulin was of no use at all, and I don't know what would have happened if the Elephant hadn't sat down squarely on the hole, blocking it up so that not a single drop of water leaked in.

"Bully for you!" cried Capt. Noah. "That's the best stunt I've seen yet!"

"It's not very comfortable," said the Elephant, with a shiver. "My, but the water's chilly!"

"Start the pumps!" commanded Capt. Noah, rushing to the foot of the companionway. "Set some of the animals to work!"

Well, after a while the Ark was pumped dry, and everybody heaved a sigh of relief.

"How long do you expect me to be a water plug?" asked the Elephant. "You don't expect me to sit here for the rest of the voyage?"

"I don't know what we'll do if you get up," answered Capt. Noah.

"Neither do I," said the Elephant.

"Let's call Mr. Jonah," said Capt. Noah.

"What's the use?" said the Elephant. "What good will he do? If he hadn't been asleep at the tiller we never would have had the accident."

"We might punish him for neglect of duty," said Capt. Noah. "We'll plug the hole up with him. He can sit on the opening for a punishment."

"Great idea!" chuckled the Elephant. "Bring him down."

So Capt. Noah hastened on deck to look for poor Mr. Jonah. And pretty soon he came back with Mr. Jonah, who of course didn't know what they were going to do with him.

"What do you want me for?" he asked. "It's pretty damp down here."

"Hello!" said the Elephant. "Excuse my not rising!"

"Certainly," said Mr. Jonah, "but you don't look very comfortable."

And then, quick as a wink, the Elephant reached out his trunk and grabbed poor Mr. Jonah.

"Help! Murder!" yelled Jonah, nearly strangled by the water, which rushed into the Ark as the Elephant got up.

"Keep quiet!" commanded Capt. Noah, and then the Elephant pushed poor Mr. Jonah into the hole.

"It's all your fault that we had this accident. Now you can stop up the leak!"

Mr. Jonah was too frightened to speak. Finally, when he partly recovered from his fright he said:

"But what am I to do?"

"Don't do a thing," said Capt. Noah, pushing him down as he started to get up. "You just sit there and be a hero!"

"I won't!" cried Mr. Jonah.

"Then we'll all drown, and you, too!" said Capt. Noah.

And just then the Weathercock shouted out loud and clear:

"Land ahead! Land ahead!"

And in a few short seconds the Ark rolled upon a sandy beach and came to a standstill.

"Throw out the anchor!" commanded Capt. Noah. "We won't take any chances this time."

And pretty soon all the animals were playing on the sand, while Mrs. Noah, with Marjorie and the boys, made a fire under some palm trees.

Suddenly Capt. Noah remembered Mr. Jonah. "Thunder and lightning!" he exclaimed, and at once descended into the hold, where he found poor Mr. Jonah still sitting on the hole in the Ark.

"Arise, noble man!" said Capt. Noah, bursting into laughter.

"Thank goodness," said Jonah. "I feel as stiff as a glass bottle stopper."

And in the next chapter you shall hear of a wonderful picnic which they all had on this little green island in the middle of the big blue ocean.

THE PICNIC

"Don't leave me alone on the Ark, Marjie, dear,

For I shall be lonely I very much fear.

Now, how would you like to be left alone

High up on a perch where the wild breezes moan?"

"The Weathercock wants to come with us," said Marjorie.

"Then why doesn't he?" said Capt. Noah, who was busily engaged in making the anchor line fast.

"I'll tell him to come with us."

And she ran up the gang-plank and called to the lonely Weathercock:

"Why don't you fly down? We'd like to have you come ashore with us."

"That's all I wanted to know," said the faithful bird. "Look out! Here she goes!"

And with a great flutter and flapping of his gilt wings he landed on the sand.

And after that he and Marjorie went over to the clump of palm trees where Mrs. Noah and the boys were resting.

"This would be a fine spot for a picnic," she said. "Did you ever go to one?"

"No, I've never been to one, although I once went to a fair with father," said Marjorie.

"Well, while the boys are busy with Capt. Noah mending the Ark, we'll get a fire started and have our lunch out here beneath the trees."

It didn't take long to get the fire started, for Mrs. Noah wished to surprise the Captain when he came back, and pretty soon the kettle was singing away:

"Hurray for the jolly picnic

And the crew of the red Noah's Ark.

I'll whistle and sing like a bird in the spring,

While the red flames gleam and spark."

"There are some nice clams on the beach," said Mrs. Noah.

So the Weathercock took a basket and went down to the water's edge and brought back enough for everybody.

And I guess Mrs. Noah had been to many a clam bake, for she knew just how to roast them in a pile of seaweed and red hot stones.

Well, pretty soon Capt. Noah with Mr. Jonah and the three boys came out of the Ark and sat down beneath the palm trees, and then all the animals sat around in a ring, for this was the first picnic they had ever been to.

"I'm as hungry as a bear," said little Marjorie, and then the Elephant began to laugh, but the bear only smiled and spread his bread with honey.

Of course, some of the animals didn't eat any of Mrs. Noah's lunch. The giraffe stood near by and ate the tender leaves off the tops of the trees and the monkeys ate cocoanuts, and the ducks and geese kept close to the water and snapped up little fishes and snails. But everybody had a wonderful time.

"I think, Mother," said Capt. Noah, wiping the crumbs from the tablecloth, and holding them out to a little brown thrush who had sat on his shoulder during the meal, "we had better spend the night ashore. I'll bring the big tent from the Ark and set it up under the trees. I'm going to do a little painting inside the Ark this afternoon."

"That's a very good idea," said Mrs. Noah.

When the tent was set up and the ropes securely fastened to the pegs which had been driven into the ground, Mrs. Noah and Marjorie busied themselves fixing it up inside in order to make it comfortable for the night.

And when evening came, a bright fire was lighted and after supper, everybody sat around and talked. Ham popped corn and Marjorie roasted apples.

"Nine o'clock," said Capt. Noah, "time for bed. We must be up early in the morning."

"It was the loveliest picnic I ever had," said Marjorie, as she kissed Mrs. Noah good night.

THE STORM

By noon the next day Capt. Noah reported that the paint was dry and the Ark ready to set sail.

"We must get the animals together," he said, looking anxiously about. "I can't imagine where they have all gone to."

"Well, I'll have everything packed and ready to put aboard by the time you round up your passengers," laughed Mrs. Noah who never seemed to worry about anything, and Marjorie thought she was the nicest person she had ever met.

"Come, boys," commanded Capt. Noah, "let's start the hunt. I hope the island isn't large, for I don't fancy walking many miles in this hot climate."

So they all started off, Mr. Jonah and the three Noah boys following Capt. Noah, and after walking for some time they came to the top of a hill, from which they had a good view of the island. And not very far away were all the animals, enjoying themselves to their hearts' content.

Capt. Noah took his bugle and blew a long blast, and at once all the animals looked around.

Then he blew again, and after that the animals formed in line with the Elephant at their head and marched toward them.

When they reached the Ark the gang-plank was lowered and they all marched aboard.

Everything below decks was in apple-pie order and the animals all seemed glad to be once more back in the Ark.

"All's well that ends well," said Capt. Noah, turning to Mr. Jonah. "My duty is to land these animals safely after the rain is over. But it looks to me as if it were going to commence again."

"There's a big black cloud in the west," shouted the Weathercock, who had flown up to his perch on the flagpole and was keeping a sharp lookout.

"Yes, I guess we're going to have some nasty weather," said Capt. Noah. "Let us hurry and get the Ark afloat."

In a few minutes the great boat was in motion, and after a short run down to the water, it once more rode the waves.

"You'd better come down to the cabin," Capt. Noah called out to the Weathercock as a flash of lightning passed across the sky. "We're going to have a storm, and you may be blown off your perch."

So the Weathercock came down and perched on his shoulder, and then he began to sing:

"Oh, the animals came into the Ark,

The little dog with a bow-wow bark,

The lion gave a kingly roar,

And the monkey shook the rat by the paw,

And the muley cow said moo-o-o,

And the rooster sang his cockle-do."

Well, it didn't take long for Capt. Noah and his crew to make everything snug and tight.

But, oh dear me! How the thunder roared and the lightning flashed, but in spite of all this, Marjorie grew so sleepy that pretty soon she went up to her little cabin with the dove on her shoulder, and crept into bed.

And then something strange happened. The Weathercock, although he had hopped into the cabin to escape the storm, went out on deck every now and then to look about him, so as to report to Capt. Noah the whereabouts of the Ark.

He didn't seem to mind the storm, for a weathercock is used to all sorts of weather and knows just from what quarter the wind is blowing, you know.

About midnight, after coming in from deck, he hopped up to little Marjorie's cabin and knocked on the door. But she was so fast asleep she didn't hear him, and if it hadn't been for the dove, who was a very light sleeper, I don't believe the Weathercock would ever have been able to tell Marjorie this strange thing that had happened.

But just as soon as the little dove heard the knocking, she flew down from her cage and opened the door. And after the Weathercock had whispered to her she went over to where Marjorie lay sound asleep in her berth.

And just then the Ark grated on something and came to a standstill, but so gradually did the great boat stop that Capt. Noah, who was also sound asleep, did not even move in his berth.

"Wake little Marjorie," whispered the Weathercock, and then the little white bird leaned over the pillow, and sang in a low voice:

"Wake up, wake up, Marjorie dear,

Come to the window,

Your home is quite near.

See, we are landed

Upon your own roof,

Just outside your bedroom.

Come, here is the proof —

I'll lift up the curtain;

There's your little bed,

With the cosy white pillow

And cover of red."

"What is it? Where am I?" asked Marjorie, opening her eyes.

"Come," said the Weathercock, "follow me."

Dreamily she got up and followed him to the window. Opposite was her own little bedroom window.

"Step over carefully," whispered the Weathercock, while the Dove took her by the hand. Marjorie stepped across the open space and entered her bedroom. Then she walked over to her own little bed and crept inside.

"Go to sleep!" whispered the Weathercock.

"See you in the morning," cooed the Dove, and with a gentle flutter they disappeared through the window. Indistinctly Marjorie heard the Ark cast away from the windowsill. And the voice of Capt. Noah came faintly to her ears:

"Careful, now! We must slip in through the nursery window without waking the household."

As the "Noah's Ark" slowly drifted in through the nursery window, Captain Noah ran forward with a hawser, ready to make fast to the book case near the big table.

"Well! Well!" he exclaimed. "It is nice to be home again!"

"It certainly is!" said Mrs. Noah, as she and the three boys came out on deck. "It is wonderful that the water has done no damage to Marjorie's pretty nursery."

"See how fast it is running away!" exclaimed Ham. "Lucky we sailed home tonight!"

Just then Mr. Noah looked at the book case. "Gee Hossephat!" he exclaimed. "See that book—'The Cruise of the Noah's Ark'—why there is my picture on the cover!"

"Look! Look!" shouted Japheth. "There are more books in the series of 'Little Journeys to Happyland!'"

"So there are," laughed Mrs. Noah. "I would like to read 'The Iceberg Express.' That sounds interesting."

"I think 'A Little Journey to Happyland in the Magic Soap Bubble' would be some trip!" exclaimed Shem.

"Time for bed," suddenly exclaimed Captain Noah. "I am going to turn out all the lights on the 'Noah's Ark.' No time tonight for you to read these other books in this series," and with these words he turned out the red light on the port side of the Ark and the green light on the starboard side and with a sigh of relief added, "Thank goodness! All the animals are well and Marjorie upstairs asleep in her little bed and the old 'Noah's Ark' back safe in the nursery."

As Captain Noah ceased speaking, the Weathercock fluttered off the Ark and over to the nursery window. Pausing a moment on the sill, he turned for one last look, and then flew straight away for Uncle Spencer's barn.

"Home again!" he chuckled.

"Who'd have thought I'd ever be

A pilot on the deep blue sea."

THE END